BUCKLEY AND THE DINOSAURS

Buckley and the Dinosaurs

The Buckley's Time Travels Series

TONY SQUIRE

S.A.Squire & T.Squire

To all lovers of Dinosaurs, and Buckley the Yowie, everywhere. Enjoy!

Bluey was quite excited today as at school he had been learning about dinosaurs. He couldn't wait to tell Buckley all about it.

Buckley was sat comfortably on the grass in front of his barn and was happy to see his friend Bluey. "Hey Buckley, guess what I've been learning about at school today?" said Bluey. Buckley shrugged his shoulders in the hope of an answer. "Dinosaurs!" exclaimed Bluey. "Dinosaurs eh? That was a long time ago. Gosh I miss them," replied Buckley, feeling a little sad, "sometimes I pop back in time to say hello, just for old time's sake you know". Bluey paused as he realised what Buckley had just said. "Hang on," said a surprised Bluey, "you can time travel?" "I can," replied Buckley, "but my magic only lets me do it a few times a month and I can stay for just five hours". "Wow, that's amazing," replied Bluey, "are you able to take a friend with you?" Buckley thought about it for a little while then asked Bluey if he was asking to go back in time. Bluey's response was lightning fast. "Yes please. Can we go now?" exclaimed Bluey.

Buckley, decided to grant Bluey's wish and, with his magic, created a time door. There was no big razzmatazz as you would expect, Buckley simply winked his eye and the magical door appeared. "Come on Bluey," said Buckley, holding open the door, "let's be off shall we?" The two friends stepped through the magic door, and as they travelled through time, it truly was a magical experience. The sensation was wonderful. They felt a rush of excitement wash over them as they were propelled through space and time, and they could feel the magic flowing through their bodies, making them tingle all over.

As they emerged on the other side of the door, they found themselves in a lush, prehistoric landscape. The colours were brighter and the air was fresher than they had ever experienced before. The sound of birds and other creatures filled the air, and they could see dinosaurs roaming around in the distance.

Buckley and Bluey looked at each other in amazement. Bluey could not believe that they were actually in the time of the dinosaurs; but they were. He felt like he and Buckley were in a dream, but it was all real. As they gazed over the land before them Bluey recognised a few of the mountains. "Look Buckley, I think we're in the Glasshouse Mountains before they became what they are today," said Bluey as he pointed at two recognisable mountains. "Yes," replied Buckley, "we may have travelled through time, but we have landed not too far away from home".

Just then they heard a sobbing noise, like someone, or some thing was crying. It was a baby woolly mammoth, which was a prehistoric elephant, who was lost and alone. The baby mammoth told them that it was looking for its mother and asked for their help. Buckley and Bluey were more than happy to lend a hand, with Bluey giving the mammoth a big hug, before they set off on an adventure to find it's mother.

As they began their quest, they came across many different types of dinosaurs, each one different and fascinating in its own way. They were amazed by the size and power of these creatures and felt honoured to be able to see them up close.

Their first stop was a lush, green forest, where they met a huge Stegosaurus, who stood at a height of fourteen feet tall, and was *twice* as long. The Stegosaurus was a plant eater, or herbivore, and lived in the forest. It had a row of large plates on its back and a spiked tail. The Stegosaurus immediately recognised Buckley. "Hello Hairy," he said, "I haven't seen you for ages". "Millions of years actually," replied Buckley, "oh, and I am known as Buckley now". "That's a good name; suits you," replied the huge dinosaur, who then realised what Buckley had just said. "What do you mean millions of years? I only saw you last week," said a confused Stegosaurus. "Last week? Cool! That means there are two Buckleys," said Bluey. "Two? Who? What is *this*?" asked the Stegosaurus, as he pointed at Bluey. "Oh this is Bluey, he is a human. They don't exist yet," replied Buckley. "Now I *am* confused," said the Stegosaurus. "I am more worried about *meeting* myself," said Buckley. The Yowie explained that he and Bluey had travelled through time from the future. "Wow!" exclaimed the Stegosaurus, "so you are not the Hairy, er Buckley, who I saw last week then?" "I am.......but I'm not.......if you know what I mean," Buckley replied. "Not really. Anyway, what brings you both here, and please Bluey, excuse my manners," said the Stegosaurus as he offered his large paw in greeting, "I am very pleased to meet you". Once they had explained Bluey's interest in dinosaurs, they informed the Stegosaurus of the baby mammoth's plight. Luckily he had seen the mother mammoth not long ago and pointed them in the direction of the swamp.

The three friends travelled to the swamp and met a giant, friendly Apatosaurus. The Apatosaurus was also a plant eater and lived in swamps and wetlands. It had a long, thick tail and a long neck and was one of the tallest dinosaurs ever, standing at fifteen feet, tall, with a huge body that was over seventy feet long. The Apatosaurus smiled and told them that it had seen the baby mammoth's mother heading towards the desert. Buckley thanked his huge friend and waved as they walked towards the edge of the sandy and dry desert.

Here, they met a Velociraptor. The Velociraptor was a carnivore, or meat eater, and lived in the desert. He wasn't very tall, and was much the same size as a fully grown human. It even walked on its hind legs, much like people do, and had a long tail and sharp claws. The Velociraptor was very helpful and told them that it had seen the baby mammoth's mother heading towards the mountains. Looking closely at Bluey, he licked his lips. "Who is your yummy friend?" he asked Buckley, "does he fancy a race? The loser can be lunch". Bluey was a little worried. "Er, there will be none of that," said Buckley as he ushered Bluey and the mammoth away.

As Buckley and Bluey continued on their journey to find the baby mammoth's mother, they came across many more different dinosaurs, a Triceratops, a Brachiosaurus, a Spinosaurus, a Pterodactyl, a Diplodocus and a Ankylosaurus, all of whom were friendly, and each one told them where they last saw the baby mammoth's mother.

The Triceratops was a herbivore and lived on the plains. It was as tall as Buckley and had a huge head, with three horns on its face, and a large frill on the back of its head. The Triceratops told them that it had seen the baby mammoth's mother heading towards the river.

At the river, they met a Brachiosaurus, who was standing in the cool water. Luckily for the trio the Brachiosaurus was also a herbivore. It had a long neck and tail and was as tall as a four storey apartment building and as long as two school buses. The Brachiosaurus told them that it had seen the baby mammoth's mother heading towards the lake.

As they reached the lake, they met a Spinosaurus. Buckley and Bluey marvelled at how huge this dinosaur was. He was at least twenty feet tall and had a face a bit like that of a crocodile. "What do *you* like to eat?" Bluey asked the huge creature. "Well, young fellow, I love meat, but don't worry as I've just had my lunch," replied the Spinosaurus, with a wink and a friendly smile. The Spinosaurus was very helpful and told them that it had seen the baby mammoth's mother heading towards the forest.

In the forest, they met a Pterodactyl. The Pterodactyl was also a meat eater and lived in the forest, and flew in the sky like a bird. It had a large wingspan and a sharp beak and was as tall as a Giraffe. The Pterodactyl told them that it had seen the baby mammoth's mother walking towards the mountains.

At the base of the mountains they met a Diplodocus. The Diplodocus was a herbivore and lived near the mountains. It had a long neck and tail and walked on four legs, and was a little bit taller than Buckley. The Diplodocus told them that it had seen the baby mammoth's mother heading towards the top of the mountain.

Finally, they met an Ankylosaurus. The Ankylosaurus was also a herbivore, and loved his vegetables and fruit. He lived near the mountain, and had a heavily armoured body and a clubbed tail. The Ankylosaurus told them that it had seen the baby mammoth's mother walking towards the tall, thin mountain just over there.

Buckley and Bluey were very grateful to all these friendly dinosaurs for helping them in their search. When they reached the tall, thin mountain, they found the baby mammoth's mother. She had been searching everywhere and was so very happy to be reunited with her baby, and thanked Buckley and Bluey for their help. Jumping for joy and cheering, Buckley and Bluey were very pleased with themselves for the good deed that they had done. Waving farewell to their new friends the pair headed off to the spot where they had arrived through the magic door.

Their five hours in the past was nearly up, and it was almost time to go home; but their adventure was not over yet, for, as they were about to leave, they were suddenly confronted by a Tyrannosaurus-Rex, or T-Rex for short. The T-Rex was a tall and terrifying creature, who stood on two legs. "You look very tasty," the T-Rex said, "who wants to be eaten first?" Bluey was very scared and hid behind Buckley. But Buckley was not afraid, for he was not only magic, but could not be harmed. "Why don't you have a good old chomp on me you big oaf?!" said Buckley, with a huge grin on his face.

Suddenly the T-Rex grabbed the Yowie in its jaws and, with his razor sharp teeth, tried to bite Buckley in half. The fearsome beast shook his head wildly, and roared loudly but, try as he may, he could not devour Buckley. In fact biting Buckley was like chewing a large rock.......impossible. The more he shook Buckley, the more Buckley laughed, for he was quite ticklish you know! The dinosaur was becoming quite angry now and bit so hard on Buckley that all of his teeth fell out, and, feeling embarrassed, as well as toothless, he dropped Buckley and ran off in to the vast forest, never to be seen again.

The excitement over, Bluey spied a cave in the side of the mountain. "I've got an idea," announced Bluey as he beckoned Buckley towards the cave, "let's leave some proof that we were here". Before leaving, with some paint made from the coloured soil, Buckley and Bluey left their hand prints on the cave wall, and wrote "Buckley and Bluey were here, from the FUTURE". "I wonder if this will ever be found?" asked Bluey. "We will find out soon enough," replied Buckley, as he winked and ushered Bluey to the time door, which had magically appeared before them.

As they stepped back through the door, they could see the world around them changing. The lush, green forests of the past gave way to the deserts and mountains of the present; whilst the creatures evolved too, their body shapes, sizes and features changing as Buckley and Bluey moved through different times in history. The dinosaurs changed into birds, and the mammals and other animals that we know today. Even though it was all happening in just a few seconds, the experience was a journey of discovery, learning, and understanding of how the world came to be. They were experiencing history in a whole new way, and it was truly magical.

Once back in the present, Buckley and Bluey felt a sense of amazement and wonder at the thought that they had travelled back in time and had met and spoken to creatures that were long gone, or extinct. They felt grateful for the exciting experience and couldn't wait to tell their friends and family all about it. There was also a surprise waiting for them. They had made the front page of many newspapers, which spoke about the discovery of a toothless T-Rex fossil, as well as their cave drawing, which had been found in the same area where they had their adventure.......millions of years ago.

They were thrilled to know that their adventure was not only a great experience for them, but had made a lasting impact on history, and that their cave drawing had been preserved for millions of years.

And so, Buckley and Bluey's adventure came to an end, but the memory of their journey through time will always be with them.

"Do you think we will travel in time again Buckley?" asked Bluey, hopefully. "I'm sure we will Bluey, I'm sure we will," replied Buckley, with a nod.

Other Books by this Author

For the pre-schooler:

'I'm Buckley and I'm a Yowie'.
'Buckley the Yowie Loves Christmas'.

For early years school children:

'Crossing the Road with Buckley the Yowie'.
'Stop Snoring Buckley!'
'It's Halloween Buckley!'
'Buckley Goes to the Beach'.
'Buckley Goes to School'.
'There is a Yowie called Buckley who Farts!'

When you get bigger you might like to read:

'Buckley the Kilcoy Yowie'.
'Buckley's Return'.
'Buckley Saves Christmas'.
'The Tale of Buckley the Yowie'.

When you get even bigger still, you might like to read:

'Buckley the Yowie and the Legend of Ned Kelly'.

About the Author

Tony Squire is the creator of Buckley, the world's favourite Yowie, who appeared in his first story, Buckley the Kilcoy Yowie, in 2019. The magical Buckley is becoming hugely popular and a series of adventures has followed, including the introduction of Buckley's friends and adopted family. Buckley has expanded from the original short stories, to a novel about Buckley's friendship with the notorious outlaw Ned Kelly, and several reading books.

Although originally intended to be a character for primary/high school children, the tales of Buckley the Yowie have become popular with younger children since the author began writing short stories and picture book readers. Buckley is fast becoming one of the best loved pre and primary school characters of all time, and his stories and adventures are enjoyed the world over.

Tony was born in November 1962, in Reading, England. Being the son of a professional soldier, he lived in five different countries, and was educated at sixteen schools worldwide. At school he particularly enjoyed history and art, which later resulted in his creation of Buckley, both in word and shape, and the insertion of his character in to real historical events. Tony's intention was always to create a fun story in which children have a both enjoyable and learning experience, whether it be about history, diversity or just plain good old fashioned morals and attitudes

The design of Buckley the Yowie was inspired by the statue of the Kilcoy Yowie in the town of Kilcoy, Queensland, Australia, which depicts the Yowie as a man, not a monster. Tony hopes that through Buckley's innocence, fun spirit, and magic, children will enjoy reading and learning at the same time.

Tony is the sole driving force in the development of all Buckley the Yowie projects at every stage.

He and his wife Sheila reside in Woolmar, Queensland, which is just outside of Kilcoy; Yowie country. Conversations and memories from their childhoods provide continual inspiration for the Buckley stories.

Tony hopes that children of all ages will grow to love his stories and pass on the love to their own children.

Ingram Content Group UK Ltd.
Milton Keynes UK
UKHW050800130323
418481UK00008B/36

9 780645 450071